Starry Forest Books, Inc. • P.O. Box 1797, 217 East 70th Street, New York, NY 10021 • Starry Forest is a trademark of Starry Forest Books, Inc. • Text and Illustrations © 2017 by Starry Forest Books, Inc. • This 2017 edition published by Starry Forest Books, Inc. • All rights reserved. No part of this publication may be reproduced, stored in a retrieval system, or transmitted in any form or by any means (including electronic, mechanical, photocopying, recording, or otherwise) without prior written permission from the publisher. • ISBN 978-1-946260-04-8 • Manufactured in Huizhou City, Guangdong Province, China • Lot #: 2 4 6 8 10 9 7 5 3 • 04/19

CLASSIC STORIES

Swan Lake

retold by
Peter Clover

illustrated by
Teresa Martinez

"*At* last! Here he comes," said the queen. "Late as usual! Even for his own birthday party."

Young Prince Siegfried leapt off his horse and bounded up the palace steps three at a time.

Royal families from across the four kingdoms had gathered at the palace for the prince's party. Many had brought along their daughters, hoping to impress the young prince. Everyone knew that the queen was looking for a suitable princess to marry her only son and heir.

Everyone watched as the queen presented Prince Siegfried
with his birthday present. It was a magnificent silver crossbow
with a prancing stag carved on its handle.

Prince Siegfried was excellent with a bow. He smiled politely,
and swung the bow across his shoulder.

The queen clapped her hands and an orchestra started playing.
The young prince mingled with the guests and forced himself to dance
with all the blushing princesses.

The princesses were of every possible shape you can imagine.
Some were tall. Some were small. One even had a moustache.

Prince Siegfried wasn't happy. He didn't want to get married, let alone choose a bride from among this birthday crowd. When he fell in love, the prince wanted it to be with someone he had chosen himself.

As darkness fell and fireworks lit up the sky,
Prince Siegfried sneaked away to be on his own.

The prince wandered away from the Royal Palace and found himself
in an enchanted forest. The prince walked for a while before stumbling upon
an unfamiliar clearing that opened onto a beautiful lake he had never seen.

Prince Siegfried sat down at the water's edge. Gentle waves lapped at
the shoreline as a fleet of white swans came gliding across the moonlit lake.

The prince noticed that one of the swans wore a golden crown. He raised his crossbow, but something about the swan made his heart jump in his chest. It was the loveliest creature he had ever seen.

The swan with the golden crown was slowly changing into a beautiful girl. Her white feathers faded into a shimmering ball gown.

Prince Siegfried thought he was dreaming
as the radiant princess stepped out of the lake
to meet him. The young prince immediately
fell in love with her. The Swan Princess told him that
her name was Odette, and that she had been bewitched
by a wicked sorcerer. All the swans were under the same spell,
and Swan Lake was filled with the tears of all the parents
who mourned for their lost daughters.

When dawn came, and the first rays of sunlight touched the water, Odette turned back into a white swan, and returned to the cold waters of Swan Lake.

Prince Siegfried had promised to meet with Odette the following night, believing that his new-found love was a secret. But Baron Von Rothbart had followed the prince to the shore of the hidden lake. The evil baron was the sorcerer who had turned Princess Odette and her maidens into swans.

The baron was afraid that Princess Odette might have found true love. Such a love would break his wicked spell over Odette. If Prince Siegfried ever declared his love for her, then Odette would be free…and become a true princess once more.

"That must never happen," whispered the baron.

The following evening was the night of the Grand Ball, where the queen expected Prince Siegfried to dance with—and choose—a future bride.

While the music played, all the prince could think about was going back to Swan Lake to be with Odette. But Baron Von Rothbart wanted his own daughter, Odile, to marry the prince. While Prince Siegfried was distracted, the baron slipped a potion into the prince's drink. The potion would make the prince believe that Odile was his true love, Odette.

Prince Siegfried could hardly believe his eyes when he saw his beautiful
Swan Princess gliding down the grand staircase. Of course it was really Odile,
but because of the magic potion, the prince saw only Odette.

Prince Siegfried asked Odile to dance, and as the young couple moved
around the floor, the queen believed her son had chosen his future bride.

"Such a pretty girl. A princess who moves with grace and charm.
The perfect choice."

The prince and princess danced, once, twice, three times and more.
And the baron watched, pleased.

Though Odile looked exactly like Odette, spoke like Odette, and moved like Odette, Prince Siegfried felt that something was wrong. He didn't feel the same magic in his heart as when he first held the Swan Princess in his arms. Something was different, but Siegfried didn't know what.

The prince looked into Odile's eyes and saw that they were black. Odette's eyes were blue. Despite this, Prince Siegfried heard himself declare his love, and ask Odile to marry him. Everyone cheered as the queen gave her royal blessing.

It was only when
Prince Siegfried glanced
toward a window that he realized he had made
a terrible mistake. The prince saw Odette on the balcony,
peering through the glass into the ballroom. Their eyes met,
and the prince's heart almost leapt out of his chest.

The prince raced outside, but Odette had gone. All Siegfried could hear was his own pounding heart, and the sound of soft beating wings overhead in the starry sky.

Prince Siegfried ran faster than he had ever run in his life. Only once did he glance back on his way to Swan Lake. When he did, he saw two dark and dangerous shapes following him. They were almost flying— like giant birds.

It was the sorcerer, Baron Von Rothbart and his evil daughter, Odile.

As the prince neared Swan Lake, he saw Princess Odette gliding away across the water. "Odette! Odette!" called Prince Siegfried. "Wait!" The Swan Princess turned her graceful neck toward him. The golden crown on her head glimmered in the moonlight. Prince Siegfried thought he saw tears falling from the swan's eyes. And his heart broke in two.

"It's no use," cried the evil baron. "You cannot win!"

"You are promised to me," screamed Odile.

But all Siegfried wanted was Odette, his beautiful Swan Princess.

"Odette, I love only you," the prince cried across the lake. And for one moment the whole world stood still. All Siegfried could see was Odette. He didn't notice the other swans turning back to maidens as the spell crumbled away. Or the baron and his daughter melting into black smoke.

As Prince Siegfried embraced Odette
in the deep water of Swan Lake, he knew
that they would always be together.